The REVENGE of TOMMY BONES

First published 2015 by A & C Black,
an imprint of Bloomsbury Publishing Plc
50 Bedford Square, London, WC1B 3DP

www.bloomsbury.com

Bloomsbury is a registered trademark of Bloomsbury Publishing Plc

A CIP catalogue for this book is available from the British Library
ISBN: 978 1 4729 1193 3

Printed and bound in Great Britain by CPI Group (UK) Ltd,
Croydon, CR0 4YY

1 3 5 7 9 10 8 6 4 2

Catch Up is a charity which
aims to address the problem of
underachievement that has its roots
in literacy and numeracy difficulties.

The REVENGE of TOMMY BONES

JULIA JARMAN

Illustrated by Sean Longcroft

A & C BLACK
AN IMPRINT OF BLOOMSBURY
LONDON   NEW DELHI   NEW YORK   SYDNEY

Contents

Chapter One

You Have Been Warned!

Ryan and Adam had missed the last bus home. It was pouring with rain.

"We can't even ring for a lift," said Ryan. "My mobile has run out."

"We'll have to walk home," groaned Adam.

"But it's pouring with rain," grumbled Ryan. "How long will it take us to walk?"

"It's only a couple of miles, if we take the short cut," said Adam.

Just then, they heard a voice in the darkness. "Don't take the short cut. D-don't walk past Tommy Bones's pond," said a shaky voice.

The boys saw an old man in the corner of the bus shelter. He had watery red eyes and he smelled of beer.

"D-don't go by Tommy Bones's pond at night," he said.

"Why not?" asked Ryan.

The wind howled. The rain came down even faster.

"If you go that way and Tommy Bones steps into the road…" The old man stopped.

Ryan laughed. "What will happen if Tommy Bones steps into the road?"

The old man got to his feet with the help of a stick. He looked at Adam and said, "You tell your mate."

Then, he left the bus shelter, muttering, "Don't say I didn't warn you."

Chapter Two

The Body in the Pond

It was even darker now. Cloud covered the moon.

"What was the old man on about?" said Ryan. "Who is Tommy Bones?"

Ryan had just moved in next door to Adam. He used to live in the town. And he was a big mouth.

Ryan asked again. "What did he mean?"

Then Ryan bent double and spoke in a shaky voice like the old man. *"If Tommy Bones steps into the road…"*

"It's a story, that's all," said Adam. "Come on, let's get going."

Ryan wouldn't shut up as they walked. He kept asking questions. "Who is Tommy Bones? Go on, tell me."

"*Was*, not *is*," said Adam at last. "He worked at Park Farm about a hundred years ago."

"What happened to him?" Ryan asked.

"He died," said Adam quietly.

"How did he die?" asked Ryan.

"He was killed," said Adam. "They found his body in the pond at Park Farm."

Ryan said, "We pass Park Farm on the way home, don't we? It's about halfway between this village and our village, isn't it?"

"Yes," said Adam. "If we take the short cut."

"How far is the other way?" Ryan asked.

"About five miles," said Adam.

"I am not walking five miles!" complained Ryan. "It will take ages."

Ryan didn't like exercise.

"It will do you good," said Adam.

But I don't understand," said Ryan, shaking his head. "We've walked past Park Farm before. We went that way last week!"

Adam nodded. "Yes, but that was in the daytime."

"Are you afraid of the dark?" asked Ryan.

"Of course not!" said Adam crossly. "But I *am* scared of seeing Tommy Bones."

Ryan's mouth fell open. "Don't be stupid!" he laughed. "He's been dead for ages. So we won't see him, will we?"

Adam stopped and looked at him. "You don't get it, do you? It's not him we see. It's his ghost."

Chapter Three

A Murder Long Ago

"You're really scared, aren't you?"
Ryan said.

Adam nodded.

Then, Ryan spoke to Adam as if he were a little kid. "Ghosts aren't real."

Adam knew that Ryan thought he was being stupid. But he had to warn him. It didn't matter what Ryan thought of him.

"OK!" said Adam crossly. "I'll tell you about Tommy Bones. When Tommy Bones was a young man, he was killed and then thrown in the pond. Now he wants revenge. He hates young men because his own youth was taken away. So he turns them into old men."

"Oh yeah?" said Ryan, trying not to smile. "And how does he do that?"

"He looks into their eyes," said Adam, with a cold shiver. "And if you look back at him you feel your skin wrinkle. Your back bends. Your hair goes white and falls out. Then your teeth…"

Now, Ryan laughed out loud. "Well, it can only happen to one of us," he said. "He can't look at both of us at the same time, can he?"

Adam went on, "And you stay like that till you die. People say that's what happened to the old man we saw in the bus shelter. Three years ago he was a teenager like us. Then the ghost looked into his eyes. That's why he was warning us."

Ryan was shaking his head. He looked at Adam as if he were being stupid. Adam *felt* stupid!

They stopped at the crossroads.

They could turn right or go straight ahead. The right-hand road meant a long walk home. The road straight ahead went past Park Farm pond.

Adam couldn't go that way, not tonight. He felt in his bones that the story was true.

It was raining even harder now. Two cars went by, spraying water. They both took the road to the right.

Adam said, "Even cars don't go there at night. Tommy Bones walks into the road, you see. Cars try to miss him and end up in the ditch. Two people have been killed like that."

Ryan just laughed.

A car slowed down beside them. There were two women in it. Adam thought he knew them.

"Let's ask for a lift," he said.

He went to tap on the driver's window but the car shot forward, along the road that went straight on.

Ryan laughed again. "Those women aren't scared of Tommy Bones."

The noise of the car got fainter.

"See," said Ryan. "Nothing happened."

Then they heard a terrible squealing sound. It was the sound of brakes being hit hard and tyres skidding.

Adam held his breath and waited for the crash.

Silence.

Then, they heard the car coming back.

Headlights rushed towards them. The car reached the crossroads and turned left without stopping, so that it went down the other road.

Adam just had time to see the faces of the women. They looked as if they had seen a ghost.

"Ryan must believe me now,"
thought Adam.

But Ryan was laughing. "Did you see their
faces? They must have scared themselves silly!"

"They must have seen him!" insisted Adam.

"There are no such things as ghosts," said
Ryan, slowly. "I'm taking the short cut."

"Sorry, mate, but I'm not," said Adam.

He hoped Ryan would come with him.
He didn't want to walk home by himself in
the dark.

But Ryan ran across the road. "Run home,
little baby! I'll tell your mummy you're on
your way!"

He started singing, "Run, run as fast as you can. Run away from the bogey man!"

Adam watched for a few minutes as Ryan set off, straight ahead.

Then he went down the right-hand road, and started to run.

Chapter Four

The Man in the Field

Ryan walked as fast as he could. Not because he was scared. He wasn't scared, but the rain was pouring down. He wanted to be warm and dry.

He wished he could go faster, but it was very dark. The moon was still behind the clouds.

He did *not* think that stupid story was true, but he wished Adam hadn't told him. He kept hearing the old man's shaky voice. "Don't say I didn't warn you."

Ryan said to himself, "Adam is a fool for believing all that rubbish. Tommy Bones is not real."

The rain stopped. It was easier to see now but there wasn't much *to* see. There were low hedges on both sides of the road and bare fields behind them. The countryside was dead boring.

Ryan was wishing he still lived in the town when ahead of him, in the dark, he saw something.

There was a man on the other side of the road.

Tommy Bones! Ryan couldn't stop the name coming into his head.

Don't look into his eyes.

Ryan looked down. He stared at his feet. Somehow, looking at his trainers make him realize how stupid he was being.

He was just imagining things. It was probably a tramp. He knew there were tramps in the country.

Ryan looked up. The man had gone.

"It must have been Adam," he thought. Adam could have cut across the field. He was tall for his age, as tall as a man.

"Adam was joking all along!" thought Ryan. "He was trying to scare me!"

Ryan swung his arms to show he wasn't scared. He started to whistle.

Adam would probably try and scare him again in a minute. Yes, there he was! Ryan could see a shape up ahead.

"I can see you!" he called.

But, when Ryan reached the place where he thought he had seen Adam, there was nobody there.

"He must be hiding somewhere," Ryan thought. He walked on, expecting Adam to jump out at him.

Ryan shouted, "I know you're there, mate!"

The moon came out from behind some clouds. Ryan could see the road ahead bending to the right. He could see Park Farm in the distance.

He came to a sudden stop.

There was a man up ahead. He was much taller than Adam.

Chapter Five

Spooked!

The man was enormous. He had long
arms and a huge head with wild, tangled hair.
Ryan felt his mouth go dry.

Don't look into his eyes.

He looked down at his own feet.

Again, the sight of his trainers made him realize how stupid he was being. He thought of Adam hiding, watching him. Laughing at him.

Ryan took a deep breath. "Stop acting like a silly kid! There are no such things as ghosts," he said to himself.

He made himself walk forward. He made himself look up at…

… a tree!

What a laugh!

Yes, the bare branches at the side did look a bit like arms. Yes, the top did look a bit like the head of a giant. But it was just a tree. That proved what the imagination could do.

Ryan walked faster. In fact he ran for a bit. It's hard to think when you're running.

He ran until the road started to go up hill. By the time he reached the top of the hill, he was puffed out.

Ryan leaned against a gatepost for a rest. He could see the road going down hill and Park Farm at the bottom. The road was flat for the rest of the way. He would be home in half an hour.

Where was Adam?

He heard a rustle. Out of the corner of his eye he saw something behind the hedge.

It wasn't Adam. It was white. It looked like a ghost!

Chapter Six

The Ghost of Tommy Bones?

Ryan couldn't take his eyes off the white thing. It was quite small. Or was it crouching? Getting ready to jump out at him?

What did Tommy Bones look like? He wished he had asked.

Don't look into his eyes.

Ryan looked down at his trainers. He felt a bit ashamed of himself as he looked at them. He had let his imagination get the better of him again.

"There are no such things as ghosts," he thought.

He took a deep breath and made himself look through the hedge.

"Baa!"

It was a sheep!

Ryan laughed. He shouted at himself. "Idiot!" Then he ran down the slope till he came to the gate of Park Farm.

He yelled as he ran. "Tommy Bones! What a name! Tommy Bones! What a laugh!" He stopped by the open gate, arms wide. "Tommy Bones! Come and get me!"

He saw someone standing in the shadow of the farmhouse.

"Adam?" called Ryan, as the figure started walking towards him.

The person seemed to melt into the darkness. "How did he do that?" thought Ryan.

Then, a voice came from behind him.

"Look into my eyes!"

Chapter Seven

The Revenge of Tommy Bones

Ryan was ready. He spun round and made a grab for Adam's shoulders.

But his hands grabbed nothing.

It wasn't Adam. It was a young man dressed in old-fashioned clothes and a flat cap. He looked like someone who had lived a hundred years ago.

He seemed to glow. Ryan told himself it was just the moonlight.

"Why would the man be in old-fashioned clothes?" Ryan tried to think of a reason. At last it came to him. It must be a scarecrow!

"You don't scare me," said Ryan. "You're just a stupid scarecrow"

"No, I am not!" said the man.

Ryan looked up at the face.

Don't look into his eyes.

The words came into Ryan's head, but it
was too late. He was looking. The young man
was looking at him. Their eyes met.

"I am the ghost of Tommy Bones!" the
man said.

Ryan tried to look back down at his feet
but he couldn't. He wanted to see his trainers
and have sensible thoughts. But he couldn't.

He couldn't take his eyes off the man's
pale face. He couldn't stop looking into the
man's eyes. They were blue with long,
pale lashes. Ryan felt them boring into
him like drills.

The man spoke softly. "It's time for Tommy's revenge."

The words made Ryan shiver. Cold ran right through him.

But it was worse than that, much worse.

Ryan felt his back bending. His head poked forward. Out of the corner of his eye he saw his hair going white.

His bones started to ache. His eyes felt sore and watery.

He looked down at his hands and saw wrinkles, brown spots and red swollen knuckles.

Something fell onto the ground in front of him. When he looked, he saw a few brown teeth and clumps of white hair.

"D-don't…" His voice sounded shaky and old. "It wasn't me. I didn't do it. It isn't fair."

But when he lifted his head there was no-one there.

Chapter Eight

Did it Really Happen?

"I fell asleep and had a nightmare."

That was what Ryan told himself as he made his way home. Ever so slowly.

"That didn't really happen."

He wanted to hurry home but it was hard to put one foot in front of the other.

"I'm not fit. I'll start going to the gym. I'll start running."

He wanted to look in a mirror and see himself looking normal. Like a teenager.

Why did he feel so out of breath?

Why was his back so bent?

Chapter Nine

The Old Man Next Door

Adam didn't get home till past midnight.

His mum was waiting up for him. "Where have you been? Why didn't you ring? I've been worried stiff."

Adam just told her they had missed the bus.

He couldn't believe that he had let that old story about Tommy Bones get to him. Ryan would tell everyone at school he'd been scared of a story.

Adam had a computer game that he knew Ryan wanted. Maybe Adam could bribe him to keep his big mouth shut.

"I'm just going round to Ryan's place," said Adam.

"Oh no, you're not!" said his mum. "You're going straight to bed. You've got school in the morning. Besides, they've got visitors. I saw Ryan's granddad arrive about half an hour ago."

"His granddad?" asked Adam.

"I think so," said his mum. "It may have been his great-granddad. He looked ever so old."

Adam tried not to think about Tommy Bones.

Chapter Ten

The Horrible Truth

In the morning, Adam was sure that the old story could not possibly be true.

But Ryan could still make everyone at school laugh at what a scaredy-cat he had been. Adam grabbed the game and rushed next door.

Ryan's mum opened the door. She looked worried.

"Hello, Adam," she said. " Ryan says he isn't going to school. Any idea what's the matter?"

"Did you see him when he got back last night?" asked Adam. "No," said Ryan's mum. "He went straight to bed."

"Is his granddad staying?" asked Adam.

Ryan's mum looked a bit surprised. "No," she said. "What made you think he might be?"

"Nothing," said Adam, as a cold chill gripped his heart.

Adam climbed the stairs slowly. He knocked on Ryan's bedroom door. "It's me, Adam," he whispered.

He heard a shuffling noise on the other side of the door. A croaky voice said, "I'm not coming out. I'm never coming out of this room."

The door opened slowly.

A bent, old man stood in front of Adam. He was bald except for a few wisps of white hair.

He stared at Adam with red watery eyes. Then he spoke in a thin shaky voice.

"I wish I had believed you!"